Herbert Allen Giles

Chinese Without a Teacher

being a collection of easy and useful sentences in the Mandarin dialect,

with a vocabulary. Second Edition

Herbert Allen Giles

Chinese Without a Teacher
being a collection of easy and useful sentences in the Mandarin dialect, with a vocabulary. Second Edition

ISBN/EAN: 9783337388850

Printed in Europe, USA, Canada, Australia, Japan

Cover: Foto ©Andreas Hilbeck / pixelio.de

More available books at **www.hansebooks.com**

無 師 自 明

CHINESE WITHOUT A TEACHER.

無 師 自 明

CHINESE
WITHOUT A TEACHER,

BEING A COLLECTION OF

EASY AND USEFUL SENTENCES

IN THE MANDARIN DIALECT.

WITH A VOCABULARY.

By HERBERT A. GILES,

H.B.M. Consul, Tamsui.

SECOND & ENLARGED EDITION.

Shanghai:

KELLY & WALSH, LIMITED, THE BUND.

SHANGHAI—HONGKONG—YOKOHAMA—SINGAPORE.

1887.

SHANGHAI :
PRINTED BY KELLY AND WALSH, LIMITED,
THE BUND AND NANKING ROAD.

Dedication.

PREFACE TO FIRST EDITION.

THE following Lessons and Vocabulary are intended to assist those who wish to acquire quickly a temporary or superficial knowledge of the Chinese language as spoken in the northern provinces, and by educated people all over the Empire.

The orthography, if such it may be called, is an attempt to express, as far as possible, Chinese sounds in simple English.

The Chinese vowel-sound *ü* is the only one which cannot be even approximately expressed, and the reader is therefore requested to pronounce it like the French *u*, or the German *ü*.

With regard to words like *shirt* or *sir*, pronounce exactly as in English, stopping short at the romanised letters, *i.e.*, not sounding them; and observe that, were it not for those romanised letters, *si* would be pronounced *sigh*, and *shi*, *shy*. Thus *ki* is to be pronounced as the *ki* in *kine*; *kwi* as the *qui* in *quite*. So, whenever *a* occurs, followed by *h*, or by *h* and other letters, the sound must be always that of the exclamation *ah!* Remember, too, that as *ow* is pronounced throughout as in the words *how* and *now*, *show* must be read in the same manner, and not *sho*, which sound is already provided for. Again, *to* is to be pronounced like one's big *toe*, and not *too*; and in *dzi*, and all words ending in *i*, the *i* is to be read like the 9th letter of the alphabet, and not *e* or any fancy sound. Above all, not like the *y* in *beauty*, that sound being itself of frequent occurrence.

Be careful to aspirate where an aspirate is required.

But to multiply observations and rules is to do the very thing it is so desirable to avoid ; I therefore leave the rest to the patience and common sense of those for whom these sentences and vocabulary have been composed.

H. A. GILES.

H.B.M's Consulate,
Tientsin, 26th October 1872.

———————

To the above it is only necessary to add that in the present edition the Chinese characters have been added, whereby it is hoped that the practical usefulness of the book will be very much enhanced.

H. A. G.

H.B.M's Consulate,
Tamsui, 1st July 1887.

INDEX.

RULES.

—:✶:—

1. Do not sound the romanised letters.

2. Wherever an apostrophe occurs, put in a strong aspirate.

3. *Ow* is to be pronounced throughout as in *how*, and *ü* as in German, or as the French *u*.

All other combinations are to be pronounced *strictly* according to the requirements of the English alphabet.

CHINESE WITHOUT A TEACHER.

THE NUMERALS.

1	一	*Yee.*
2	二 or 兩	*Ur* or *layang* or *layah.*
3	三	*Sah* or *sahn.*
4	四	*Sir.*
5	五	*Woo.*
6	六	*Layo.*
7	七	*Ch'ee.*
8	八	*Pah.*
9	九	*Cheeoo.*
10	十	*Shirt.*
11	十一	*Shirtyee.*
12	十二	*Shirtur.*
13	十三	*Shirtsahn.*
20	二十	*Urshirt.*
26	二十六	*Urshirtlayo.*

30	三十	*Sahnshirt.*
37	八十七	*Pahshirtch'ee.*
91	九十一	*Cheeooshirtyee.*
100	一百	*Yee pi.*
101	一百零一	*Yee pi ling yee.*
110	一百一十	*Yee pi yee shirt.*
112	一百一十二	*Yee pi yeeshirt ur.*
120	一百二十	*Yee pi urshirt.*
200	二百	*Ur pi.*
340	三百四十	*Sahn pi sirshirt.*
561	五百六十一	*Woo pi layo shirtyee.*
922	九百二十二	*Cheeoo pi urshirt ur.*
1,000	一千	*Yee ch'e-enn.*
1,010	一千零一十	*Yee ch'e-enn ling yee-shirt.*
10,000	一萬	*Yee wahn.*
100,000	十萬	*Shirt wahn.*

THE TOURIST.

Come!	來	*Li!*
Come here!	這兒來	*Cher li!*
Make haste!	快快	*K'wi k'wi!*
Why don't you come?	你爲甚麽不來	*Nee way shummo poo li?*
I can't wait	我不能等	*Woa poo nung tung.*
It's getting late	天不早	*T'e-enn poo dzow.*
I want to be off	我要走	*Woa yow dzo.*
Where are you going?	你上那兒	*Nee shahng nar?*
To Peking	我上北京去	*Woa shahng Payching.*
When do you start?	你多喀起身	*Nee toa dzahn ch'ee shun?*
I start to-day	我今天起身	*Woa chint'e-enn ch'ee shun.*
Have you hired your carts?	你僱了車沒有	*Nee koolayow ch'aw ma-yo?*
I am going by boat	我坐船	*Woa dzoa ch'wahn.*
Boy! hire two boats	來, 僱兩隻船	*Boy! koo layangchirp ch'wahn.*
How much does the boatman want?	船戶要多少錢	*Chwahnhoo yow toa show ch'e-enn?*
Seven dollars	七塊洋錢	*Ch'ee k'wi ch'e-enn?*
This isn't a good boat	這個船不好	*Chayka ch'wahn poo how.*
How far are we from Peking?	北京離這兒多遠	*Payching lee cher toa yüahn?*

Is my baggage stowed away on board?	行李都裝在船上沒有	Shing-lee to jwong-dzi ch'wahn-shahng ma-yo?
How many boxes are there?	有多少箱	Yo toa show sheeangdza?
When shall we get to Peking?	今兒到北京	Chee-er tow Payching?
It isn't certain	不一定	Poo yee ting.
Is the wind fair?	有順風沒有	Yo shoon fung mayo?
How many boatmen are there?	有多少水手	Yo toa show shooey-sho?
I shall go by cart	我要坐車	Woa yow dzoa ch'aw.
We shall be quicker by road	旱路快	Hahn-loo k'wi.
This cart is dirty	這個車朧臢	Chayka ch'aw ah-dzah.
Your animals are bad	你的生口不好	Neety shungk'o poo how.
What's your name? (1) To an inferior (2) To an equal	(1) 你姓甚麼 (2) 貴姓	(1) Nee shing shummo? (2) Kway shing?
I'll give you five dollars	我給你五塊洋錢	Woa kay nee woo k'wi ch'e-enn.
I'll give you wine-money besides	還要給你酒錢	Hi yow kay nee cheeoo ch'e-enn.
Go on quickly!	快走罷	K'wi dzo-pah!
Call my servant	叫跟班的來	Cheeow kunpahnty li.
Has he come back?	他回來的沒有	T'ah hooey-li-la mayo?
I want to wash my face	我要洗臉	Woa yow shee lay-enn.
Bring some water	拿水來	Nah shooey li.
I don't want hot water	不要熱水	Poo yow raw shooey.
Bring me a piece of soap	擎一塊胰子	Nah yee k'wi yeedza.
I haven't a towel	沒有手巾	Mayo sho-cheen.

It's all in the bag	都在口袋裏頭	*To dzi k'o-ti lee-t'o.*
Shut the window	關上窓糊 尸	*Kwahn-shahng ch'wong-hoo.*
Open the door	開門	*K'i mun.*
Pour me out a glass of water	給我倒一杯水	*Kay woa tow yee pay shoowy.*
Get me a chair [not a sedan]	拿一張椅子	*Nah ye jahng yeedza.*
Bring me a light	拏火來	*Nah hwaw li.*
Make a fire	弄火	*Loong hwaw.*
Bring me a cigar	拏烟捲兒來	*Nah yen-chüar li.*
I want to have chow-chow now	現在要吃飯	*Shendzi yow ch'irp fahn.*
I want beef; I don't want pork	要牛肉不要猪肉	*Yow new-ro; poo yow joo-ro.*
Is there good mutton to be had?	有好羊肉沒有	*Yo how yahng-ro mayo?*
I also want some fruit	還要菓子	*Ili yow kwo-dza.*
Have you any bread?	有麵包沒有	*Yo me-enpow mayo?*
Bring the potatoes	拏山藥豆兒	*Nah shahn-yow-tor.*
Open a bottle of wine	開一瓶酒	*K'i yee p'ing cheewo.*
Where's the corkscrew?	螺絲在那兒	*Law-saw dzi nar?*
Make some tea	起茶	*Ch'ee ch'ah.*
Bring me a tea-cup	拏茶碗來	*Nah ch'ah-wahn li.*
Put that outside	把這個擱在外頭	*Pah chayka, kawdzi wi-t'o.*
I don't want this	不要這個	*Poo yow chayka.*

That's not good	那個不好·	*Nahka poo how.*
This plate is dirty	這個盤子腌臜	*Chayka p'ahndza ah-dzah.*
Get me a clean one	換一個新的	*Hwahn yeeka sheenty.*
Bring me a knife	拏一把刀子	*Nah yee pah towdza.*
Bring me a fork	拏一把錹子	*Nah yee pah ch'ahdza.*

THE MERCHANT.

Ask the compradore to come.	請買辦來	*Ch'ing mi-pahn li.*
Who are you?	你是甚麼人	*Nee shirt shummo ren?*
What are you doing?	你做甚麼	*Nee dzoa shummo?*
I keep the accounts	我算賬	*Woa sooahn jahng.*
How many hands do you employ in the hong?	行裏用多少人	*Hahng-lee yoong toa show ren?*
Fifty men are too many	五十人太多	*Woo-shirt ren t'i toa.*
The business is not large	買賣不大	*Mi-mi poo tah.*
Hire ten more men	再僱十個人	*Dzi koo shirtka ren.*
A steamer has come	輪船來咯	*Loon ch'wahn li-la.*
Has it come up to the jetty?	到了馬頭沒有	*Towla maht'o mayo?*
What steamer is it?	是甚麼輪船	*Shirt shummo loon ch'wahn?*
What cargo is there on board?	船上裝甚麼貨	*Ch'wahn-shahng jwong shummo hwaw?*
There are 200 bales Grey Shirtings	有二百疋洋布	*Yo ur pi p'ee yahng-poo.*
Is there any Opium?	有洋藥沒有	*Yo yahng-yow mayo?*
Put it in the godown	擱在棧房裡	*Kawdzi jahn-fahnglee.*
Hire four cargo-boats	僱四隻駁船	*Koo sir chirp paw ch'wahn.*
The steamer leaves to-morrow	輪船明天開行	*Loon ch'wahn mingt'e-enn k'i shing.*

At what o'clock ?	幾點鐘	Chee te-enn-joong.
At half-past eight in the morning	八點半鐘	Pah te-enn pahn-joong.
This steamer is very fast	這個輪船狠快	Chayka loon ch'wahn hun k'wi.
The cabins are also very good	客艙也狠好	K'aw-ts'ahng yay hun how.
What is the fare from here to Shanghai ?	打這兒到上海得多少錢	Tah-cher tow Shahng-hi tay toa show ch'e-enn?
Twenty taels	二十兩銀子	Urshirt layang yeendza.
Food is provided on board	船上管飯	Ch'wahn-shahng kooahn fahn.
Where's the captain ?	船主在那兒	Ch'wahn-joo dzi nar ?
The captain has gone to the Consulate.	船主上領事官衙門	Ch'wahn-joo shahng ling-shirt-kwahn yahmun.
When will he be back ?	多咱回來	Toa-dzahn hooey-li?
In a very short time	一會兒就來	E-hwer cheeoo-li.
Take a seat	請坐	Ch'ing dzoa.
What's in this ?	這裡頭有甚麼	Chaw lee-t'o yo shummo?
I don't know	我不知道	Woa poo-che-tow.
I'll come again to-morrow	我明天回來	Woa mingt'e-enn hooey-li.
Where is the "Customs" ?	海關在那兒	Hi-kwahn dzi nar ?
Send this to the "Pow-shoon" hong	送寶順洋行	Soong "Pow-shoon" yahng hahng.
Where does this letter come from ?	這一封信是那兒來的	Chay-yee-fung-sheen shirt nar li-ty?
There's no answer	沒有回信	Mayo hooey sheen.

He needn't wait	他不用等	T'ah poo yoong tung.
Bring me a pen and ink	拏筆墨來	Nah pee-maw li.
I don't want Chinese pens and ink	不要中國筆墨	Poo yow choong-kwo pec-maw.
Bring me a sheet of paper	拏一張紙	Nah yee jahng jump.
Have all the letters come?	信都來沒有	Sheen to li-la mayo?
Who's that man outside?	外頭那個人是誰	Wi-t'o negga ren shirt shooey?
It's Mr.—of the "Kwong-loong" hong	廣隆東家	Kwong-loong toong-cheeah.
Ask him to come in	請他進來	Ch'ing t'ah cheen-li.
Ask the compradore if these notes are good	問買辦這個票子好不好	Wun mi-pahn, chayka p'eeowdza how-poo-how
I have 1,000 piculs of rice	我有一千担白米	Woa yo yee ch'e-enn tahn pi-mee.
I want $3.00 per picul	每一担要三塊洋錢	May yee tahn, yow sahn k'wi ch'e-enn.
Too dear	太貴	T'i kooey.
Can't let you have it for less	少咯不賣	Showla poo mi.
Come and look at it	你來看看	Nee li k'ahn-e-k'ahn.
Have you any coal?	你有煤沒有	Nee yo may mayo?
I'll write to you to-morrow	我明天給你寫信	Woa mingt'e-enn kay nee seeay sheen.
To-morrow is Sunday	明天禮拜	Mingt'e-enn lee-pi.
Send a man	打發一個人來	Tahfah yeeka ren li.
Wait a little; I'll go myself	等一等我自己去	Tung-e-tung; woa adze-chee ch'ü.

You needn't come	你不用來	*Nee poo yoong li.*
What else do you want?	你還要甚麼	*Nee hi yow shummo?*
I don't want anything	我不要甚麼	*Woa poo yow shummo.*
Where's your master?	你的東家在那兒	*Neety toong-cheeah dzi nar?*
He's in the office	在寫字房	*Dzi seeaydzafahng.*
I am going out now	現在我要出門	*Shendzi woa yow ch'oo mun.*
I am going to the "Customs"	我上海關	*Woa shahng Hi-kwahn.*
The Commissioner of Customs has come	稅務司來咯	*Shooey-woo-sir li-la.*
The pilot is on board, waiting	引水的在船上等着	*Yeen - shooeyty dzi ch'wahn-shahng tungja.*

GENERAL.

Where's my watch ?	我的錶在那兒	Woaty peeow dzi nar?
Hire a sedan-chair	僱一頂橋子	Koo yee ting cheeowdza.
Bring the key	拏鑰匙	Nah yowsh.
Call the carpenter	叫木匠來	Cheeow moocheeang li.
This nail must be pulled out	這個釘子要拔起來	Chayka tingdza yow pah-ch'ee-li.
I want it coloured	要刷色	Yow shwah si.
I want this box opened (if nailed down)	這個箱子要撬開	Chayka sheeangdza yow ch'eeow-k'i.
Solder it down	拏錫臘釬上	Nah sheelah hahnshahng
Buy 5 lbs. of cotton-wool	你買五斤棉花	Nee mi woo-cheen me-enhwah.
This tea-cup is broken	這個茶碗破咯	Chayka ch'ahwahn p'awla.
Send for the tinker	我一個鏒碗的	Chow yeeka chü-wahuty.
This door is cracked	這個門裂咯	Chayka mun leeayla.
Is this water filtered ?	這個水過淋沒有	Chayka shooey kwo leen mayo?
Who is this gentleman ?	這一位是誰	Chay yee way, shirt shooey?
Is it raining ?	下雨不下雨	Seeah-yü poo seeah-yü?
It is sure to blow to-day	今天必要颱風	Chint'e-enn pee yow kwah fung.
The river will soon freeze	快要封河	K'wi yow fung haw.
Have you a skin coat ?	你有皮袄沒有	Nee yo p'ce-ow mayo?

It's very cold in the north	北邊兒狠冷	*Paype-er hun lung.*
Tell the coolie to paste up the windows	叫僱力糊上窓糊	*Checow coolie hooshahng ch'wonghoo.*
Next week I want to get the matting up.	下禮拜要打篷子	*Secah lee-pi yow tah p'ungdza.*
The mosquitoes are very bad this year	今年蚊子狠利害	*Chin-ne-enn, wundza hun lee-hi.*
I have no umbrella	我沒有雨傘	*Woa mayo yü-sahn.*
What are you afraid of ?	怕甚麼	*P'ah shummo?*
I am afraid of sun-stroke	怕晒咯	*P'ah shi-la.*
Foreign articles are all very good	外國東西都好	*Wi-kwo toongshee to how*
This room leaks (from rain)	這個屋子漏	*Chayka woodza lo.*
Get a lantern	打燈籠	*Tah tungloong.*
Don't tell lies	你別撒謊	*Nee peeay sah-hwong.*
Have you a father and mother ?	你有父母沒有	*Nee yo foo-moo mayo?*
Tell him to wait	叫他等一等	*Cheeow t'ah tung-e-tung.*
I haven't got leisure now (to do anything)	現在我沒有工夫	*Shendzi woa mayo koong-foo.*

THE HOUSEWIFE.

Light the lamp	點燈	*Te-enn tung.*
Call the cook	叫厨子來	*Cheeow ch'oodza li.*
I want to take the accounts now	現在要算賬	*Shendzi yow sooahn jahng.*
Your bill is all right	你的賬目不錯	*Neety jahngmoo poo ts'oa*
I'll pay you to-morrow	我明天給你錢	*Woa mingt'e-enn kay nce ch'e-enn.*
I shall have a dinner-party to-morrow night	明天晚上要請客	*Mingt'e-enn wahn-shahng yow ch'ing k'aw*
Roast a leg of mutton	烤一個羊腿	*K'ow yeeka yahng-t'ooey.*
Boil a piece of salt beef	煮一塊鹹牛肉	*Joo yee k'wi se-enn new-ro.*
Is there any fish to be got?	有魚肉沒有	*Yo yü-ro mayo?*
I want four kinds of sweets	要四樣兒點心	*Yow sir yahnger te-en-sheen.*
Roast two pheasants	烤兩個野雞	*K'ow layanga yay-chee.*
I don't want any ducks	不要鴨子	*Poo yow yahdza.*
These eggs are bad	這個雞子兒不好	*Chayka cheedzer poo how.*
Buy a bottle of milk	買一瓶奶子	*Mi yee p'ing ni-dza.*
Fry several pieces of bread	炸幾塊麵包	*Jah chee k'wi me-enpow.*
Don't use pork-fat for frying them; use beef-fat	不要拏猪油炸拏牛油炸	*Poa yow nah joo-yo jah; nah new-yo.*

To-day I want hare soup	今天要野兎湯	*Chint'e-enn yow yay-mow t'ahng.*
Tell the cook to make chicken broth	呌厨子做鷄湯	*Cheeow ch'oodza dzo chee t'ahng.*
Is it ready?	得咯沒有	*Tawla mayo?*
This cook is not a good one	這個厨子不好	*Chayka ch'oodza poo how*
The coolie is also very lazy	僱力也狠懶惰	*Coolie yay hun lahn taw.*
Where's the amah?	老媽兒在那兒	*Low-mar dzi nar?*
I want my hair done now	現在要梳頭	*Shendzi yow shoo t'o.*
These clothes must be washed	這個衣裳要洗一洗	*Chayka eeshahng yow shee-e-shee.*
Don't put any soda in the water	水裡不要擱鹼	*Shooey-lee poo yow kaw je-enn.*
Has the washerman come?	洗衣裳的來沒有	*Shee eeshahngty li-la mayo?*
How many pieces are there this month?	這個月有多少件衣裳	*Chayka yüay yo toa show je-enn eeshang?*
Every hundred pieces $3.00	每一百件三塊洋錢	*May yee pi je-enn, sahn-k'wi-ch'e-enn.*
He hasn't washed this one clean	這個他沒洗乾淨	*Chayka, t'ah may shee kahn-ching.*
I must fine him a dollar	我要跑他一塊洋錢	*Woa yow p'ow t'ah yee-k'wi-ch'e-enn.*
Here are your wages	這是你的工錢	*Cha shirt neety koong-ch'e-enn.*
Get me a tailor	找一個裁縫	*Chow yeeka ts'i-fung.*

Tell the coolie to clean up the room	叫僱力拾得屋子	*Cheeow coolie shirttaw woodza.*
You must wash the floor	地板要洗一洗	*Tee-pahn yow shec-e-shee*
You must rub the table	桌子耍擦一擦	*Chawdza yow ts'ah-e-ts'ah.*
Bring a feather-brush	拏担子來	*Nah tahndza li.*
Now I want to put up the stove	現在要打爐子	*Shendzi yow tah loodza.*
You must first brush it	先要刷一刷	*Shen yow shwah-e-shwah*
Have you any black-lead?	有黑麪沒有	*Yo hay me-enn mayo?*
This brush won't do	這個刷子不行	*Chayka shwahdza poo shing.*
The chimney is stopped up	烟桶子社住咯	*Yen t'oongdza too-choola.*
There must be soot in it	裡頭必有烟煤子	*Leet'o pee yo yen-may-dza.*
We must think of some way to clean it	得想法子拾得	*Tay sheeahng fahdza shirttaw.*
This stove smokes	這個爐子冒烟	*Chayka loodza mow yen.*
Buy a picul of Chinese coal	叫一擔本地米	*Cheeow yee tahn pun-tee may.*
Also 30 catties of char-coal	還要三十觔炭	*Hi yow sahnshirt-cheen t'ahn.*
Have you bought the fire-wood?	你買咯劈柴沒有	*Nee mi-la p'ee-ch'i mayo?*
I want this put in the ice-box	這個耍下在氷箱子裡	*Chayka yow seeahdzi ping-sheeangdza-lee.*
Tell the cook to make a bowl of arrowroot	叫廚子冲一碗藕粉	*Cheeow ch'oodza ch'oong yee wahn o-fun.*
Thicker than he made it yesterday	比昨天要稠	*Pee dzoa-t'e-enn yow ch'o*
Bring some boiling wa-ter	拏開水來	*Nah k'i shooey li.*

Warm water won't do; I want it boiling	温和水不行要熟水	*Wunhaw shooey pushing; yow raw shooey.*
I am not very well to-day	今日我不舒服	*Chint'e-enn woa poo shoo-foo.*
What's the matter?	怎麼樣	*Dzummo-yahng?*
I've got fever and ague	發瘧子	*Woa fah-yowdza.*
I'll give you a dose of medicine	我給你一服藥	*Woa kay nce yee foo yow.*
I want to buy a pound of camphor	要買一觔樟腦	*Yow mi yee-cheen ch'ow-now.*
Take this out and shake it (of clothes)	拏外頭抖落抖落	*Nah wi-t'o, tolo tolo.*
Brush these shoes	把這個鞋刷一刷	*Pah chayka sceay, shwah-e-shwah.*
Take this and spread it on the top (of blankets, etc.)	把這個舖在上頭	*Pah chayka, p'oodzi shahngt'o.*
Tuck this in under	把這個壓在地下	*Pah chayka yahdzi teesceah.*
I don't want to wear that hat to-day	今天不要載那個帽子	*Chint'e-cnn poo yow ti nahka mowdza.*
Is my apron made yet?	你的圍裙做完了沒有	*Woa-ty way-ch'ün dzoa wahnla mayo?*
Mend these stockings	縫這個襪子	*Fung chaykaw wahdza.*
Tell the amah to get up	叫老媽起來	*Cheeow lowmar ch'ee-li.*
Why are you so late?	你爲甚麼這麼晚	*Nce way shummo chummo wahn?*
Don't you go to sleep	你別睡覺	*Nee peeay shooey-cheeow.*
There's no one to carry the baby	沒人抱孩子	*May ren pow hi-dzi.*
Where have you been?	你打那兒回來	*Nee tah nar hooeyli?*

Don't chew betel-nut	你別吃檳榔	*Nee peeay ch'irp ping-lahng.*
Fetch my gloves	拏我的手套兒來	*Nah woaty sho-t'owr li.*
They are in the drawer	在抽屜裡頭	*Dzi ch'o-t'ee leet'o.*
Is the cupboard (or ward-robe) locked?	櫃子鎖了沒有	*Kweydza sawla mayo?*
I am going out	我要出門	*Woa yow ch'oo mun.*
You look after the house	你看守門戶	*Nee k'ahn-sho munhoo.*
Bring the small looking-glass	拏小鏡子來	*Nah sheeow jingdza li.*
Bring the wash-hand basin	拏臉盆來	*Nah layenn-p'un li.*
Pour this water out	把這個水倒咯	*Pah chayka shooey towla*
Your shoes are down at heel	你的鞋趿垃着	*Neety seeay sahlahja.*
It's not proper (respect-ful)	不是樣子	*Poo shirt yahngdza.*
You haven't brushed your hair to-day	今天你沒疏頭	*Chint'e-enn nee may shoo t'o.*
Why are you so idle?	你為甚麼這麼懶惰	*Nee way shummo chum-mo lahntaw?*
Look out for another situation	你找一個別的事	*Nee chow yeeka peeayty shirt.*
Come again at the end of the month	月底再來	*Yüay tee dzi li.*
I want this mattress co-vered (with new stuff)	這個褥子要幔上	*Chayka roodza yow mahnshahng.*
Open this bundle	這個包服要打開	*Chayka powfoo yow tahk'i.*
Bring a flat-iron	拏烙鐵來	*Nah lowt'y li.*

I want to iron the creases out of the clothes	衣裳摺兒要熨開	*Eeshahng-chawr yow yünk'i.*
Tell the tailor to make a mosquito-curtain	叫裁縫做一個蚊帳	*Cheeow ts'i-fung dzoa yeeka wun-jahng.*
These sheets havn't been washed clean	這被單沒洗乾淨	*Chayka pay-tahn may shee kahnching.*
Put this in hot water to soak	把這個擱在熱水裡發開	*Pah chayka kawdzi raw shooeylee fahk'i.*
Bring me a pillow	拏枕頭來	*Nah chunt'o li.*
Where's the cushion?	椅墊子在那兒	*E-tee-endza dzi nar?*
Put this on the book-case	擱在書架子上	*Kawdzi shoo-chee-ahdza-shahng.*
Don't leave the house	你別出門	*Nee peeay ch'oo mun.*
Take care *or* be careful	小心	*Sheeow sheen.*

THE SPORTSMAN.

Saddle the pony	背馬	*Pay mah*
Where are the dogs?	狗在那兒	*Ko dzi nar?*
Call the mahfoo	叫馬夫來	*Cheeow mahfoo li*
I don't want this saddle	不要這個鞍子	*Poo yow chayka ahndza*
Bring the bridle	拏嚼子來	*Na cheeowdza li*
There's no halter	沒有籠頭	*Mayo loongt'o*
This stirrup is too long	這個馬鐙長	*Chayka mahtung ch'ahng*
That one is too short	那個馬鐙短	*Nahka mahtung tooahn*
Bring my whip	拏鞭子來	*Nah pe-endza li*
I want to ride the bay pony	我要騎紅馬	*Woa yow ch'ee hoong mah*
I'll ride the white pony to-morrow	明天要騎白馬	*Mingt'e-enn yow ch'ee pi mah*
You haven't fed him	你沒有餵他	*Nee mayo way t'ah*
You only give him chopped straw	你竟給他短草	*Nee jing kay t'ah too-un ts'ow*
You must also give him Indian corn	你還得給他棒子	*Nee hi tay kay t'ah pahngdza*
Bring a bucket of water	拏--筲水	*Nah yee show shooey*
This girth won't do	這個肚帶不行	*Chayka too-ti poo shing*
Get a fresh one	換一個新的	*Hwahn yeeka sheenty*
Get him shod to-morrow	明天給他釘掌	*Mingt'e-enn kay t'ah ting jahng*

This stable is draughty	這個馬棚透風	*Chayka mahp'ung t'o fung*
You must put a pane of glass here	這兒娶配一塊玻璃	*Cher yow p'ay yeck'wi pawlee*
Feed the dogs	餵狗	*Way ko*
Where's the big dog?	大狗在那兒	*Tah ko dzi nar?*
The small dog hasn't come back	小狗沒回來	*Sheeow ko may hooey-li.*
Are there any hares here?	這個地方有野貓沒有	*Chayka teefahng yo yay-mow mayo?*
Are there any foxes?	有狐狸沒有	*Yo hoolee mayo?*
The pony is hot; don't feed him yet	馬出了汗先不要狠他	*Mah ch'oola hahn; shen poo yow way t'ah.*
I want to buy a good pony	我要買一疋好馬	*Woa yow mi yee p'ee how mah.*
This pony isn't fast, or, won't do for racing	這個馬跑得不快	*Chayka mah, p'owta poo k'wi.*
A good pony is very dear now	好馬現在狠貴	*How mah shendzi hun kooey.*
Are there any wolves here?	這兒有狼沒有	*Cher yo lahng mayo?*
Walk my pony about	把馬蹓一蹓	*Pah mah layo-layo.*
A fox! a fox! Let go the dogs!	狐狸狐狸放狗放狗	*Hoolee! hoolee! Fahng ko, fahng ko!*

IN A SHOP.

Have you any good skins here?	你們這兒有好皮子沒有	Neemun-cher yo how p'eedza mayo?
What kind do you want?	你要甚麼樣兒皮子	Nee yow shummo yahnger pee'dza?
I want sable	要貂鼠皮	Yow teeow-sho p'ee.
This jacket is Tls. 150.00	這個馬褂一百五十兩銀子	Chayka mahkwah yee pi wooshirt layang yeendza.
Have you a tiger-skin?	有老狐皮沒有	Yo lowhoo-p'ee mayo?
The hair is not long	毛不長	Mow poo ch'ahng.
What skin is this jacket made of?	這個馬褂是甚麼皮子	Chaykaw mahkwah shirt shummo p'eedza?
Squirrel	灰鼠	Hwey-shoo.
I don't want it made up	不要現成兒的	Poo yow shen-ch'unger-ty.
I want it in pieces	要碎塊兒的	Yow sooey-k'warty.
(Looking at the leather side). It's not well made up	板子不好	Pahndza poo how.
It's not a good skin	不是好皮子	Poo shirt how p'eedza.
Have you any sea-otter?	有海虎沒有	Yo hi-foo mayo?
Bring some black astracan	拏黑子羔	Nah hay-adze-kow.
I don't want a jacket; I want a robe	不要馬褂要外套兒	Poo yow mahkwah; yow wi-t'owr.
Have you any unborn lamb-skin?	有草上霜沒有	Yo ts'ow-shahng-shwong mayo?

This is too dear	這個太貴	Chayka t'i kooey.
Can't let you have it for less	少咯不賣	Showla poo mi.
I'll come back to-morrow	我明天回來	Woa mingt'e-enn hooey-li.
This is a cat-skin	這是猫皮	Chaw shirt mow p'ee.
Is it dyed?	染過沒染過	Rahnkwo may-rahnkwo?
The quality is not good	成色不好	Ch'ung-saw poo how.
Make me a fur cap	給我做一個皮帽子	Kay woa dzoa yceka p'ee mowdza.
I'll give you $5.00	我給你五塊洋錢	Woa kay nee woo-k'wi-ch'e-een.
When will it be finished?	多喒做完咯	Toa-dzahn dzoa wahnla?
Inside I want red silk	裡面兒要紅綢子	Leemyer yow hoong ch'o-dza.
Make it like this pattern	照着這個樣兒做	Chowja chayka yahnger dzoa.
A little bigger than this	比這個大點兒	Pee chayka tah te-er.
I don't want anything else	不要別的	Poo yow peeayty.
How much do you want for this?	這個你要多少錢	Chayka, nee yow toa-show-ch'e-enn?
Speak the truth, now!	你說實話	Nee shwo shirt hwah.
I won't buy any of your things	不要買你的東西	Poo yow mi neety toong-shee.

THE SAILOR.

This is a steamer	這個是輪船	Chayka shirt loon ch'wahn.
That is a sailing-vessel	那個是艙舨船	Nahka shirt cheeahpohn ch'wahn.
Is this a screw or a paddle-steamer ?	這個船是暗輪是明輪	Chayka ch'wahn shirt ahn-loon, shirt ming-loon?
Steamers don't need sails	輪船不用打篷	Loon ch'wahn poo ywong tah p'ung.
Where is the steersman ?	舵工在那兒	Toa-koong dzi nar?
He's in the hold or down below	在艙裏頭	Dzi ts'ahng-leet'o.
How much coal do you burn in a day ?	一天燒多少煤	Yee t'e-enn show toa-show may?
We go 10 knots an hour	一點鐘走三十里	Yee te-enn joong dzow sahnshirt lee.
That's not very fast	不算狠快	Poo soon hun k'wi.
The steamer's aground	輪船淺住了	Loon ch'wahn ch'e-enn-joola.
That doesn't matter	不要緊	Poo yow cheen.
Is it flood-tide or ebb-tide now ?	現在是漲潮是溶潮	Shendzi shirt chahng-ch'ow, shirt low-ch'ow?
Where's the bar?	欄江沙在那兒	Lahn-cheeang-shah dzi nar?
This ship has three masts	這個船有三枝桅杆	Chayka ch'wahn yo sahn chirp waykahn.
Chinese junks are clumsy things	中國船笨	Choongkwo ch'wahn pun.
Foreign ships are made of iron	外國船是鐵做的	Wi-kwo ch'wahn shirt t'eeay dzoaty.
There are ships both of iron and wood	有鐵做的有木頭做的	Yo t'eeay dzoaty, yo moot'o dzoaty.

What's this?	這個是甚麼	*Chayka shirt shummo?*
This is the compass	這個是定南針	*Chayka shirt ting-nahn-chun.*
The saloon is here	客艙在這兒	*K'aw-ts'ahng dzi cher.*
Don't you find it clean?	乾淨不乾淨	*Kahnching poo kahn-ching?*
Are you sea-sick?	暈船不暈船	*Yün-ch'wahn poo yün-ch'wahn?*
We shall get into port to-morrow	明天進口	*Mingt'e-enn cheen k'o.*
Have you had chow-chow?	吃了飯沒有	*Ch'irpla-fahn mayo?*
This telescope (or glasses) is mine	這個千里眼是我的	*Chayka ch'e-enlecyenn shirt woaty.*
This is a thermometer	這個是寒暑錶	*Chayka shirt hahnshoo-peeow.*
I want to get this line out	這個繩子要拋開	*Chayka shungdza yow p'ow-k'i.*
Don't let go the anchor	不要下錨	*Poo yow seeah mow.*
Make fast!	繞住	*Row choo!*
Let go!	鬆 鬆手	*Soong or soong sho!*
These bends are not easy to go round	這個河灣不好轉	*Chayka haw-wahn poo how chooahn.*
There's a junk in the middle of the river	當河有一個中國船	*Dahng-haw yo yceka choong-kwo ch'wahn.*

GENERAL.

Do you know this man?	這個人你認得不認得	*Chayka ren nee renta-poo-renta?*
Where does he live?	他在那兒住	*T'ah dzi nar choo?*
He's a southerner	他是南邊人	*T'ah shirt nahnpe-enn ren.*
I don't like him	我不喜歡他	*Woa poo sheehwahn t'ah*
He can't be depended upon	靠不住	*K'ow poo choo.*
You mind your own business	你幹你的	*Nec kahn neety.*
Where's my ring?	我的鑒子在那兒	*Woaty layo-dza dzi nar?*
It's lost	丟咯	*Te-ola.*
It can't be lost	不能丟咯	*Poo nung te-ola.*
It's probably in the bed-room	大概在睡覺屋裡	*Tah-ki dzi shooey-cheeowty woolee.*
Every morning I want to bathe	天天早起要洗澡	*T'e-enn t'e-enn dzowch'ee yow shee-dzow.*
Bring well-water; I don't want river-water	擎井水不要河水	*Nah ching-shooey; poo yow haw-shooey.*
Have you a lead-pencil?	你有鉛筆沒有	*Nee yo ch'e-en pee mayo?*
I have a head-ache	我腦袋痛	*Woa now-ti t'ung.*
What is the day of the month?	今兒幾兒咯	*Cheer cheerla?*
To-day is the 5th	今兒初五 or 今天初五	*Cheer ch'oo woo or cheen-t'e-enn ch'oo woo.*

To-morrow is the 29th	明天二十九	Mingt'e-enn urshirt cheeoo.
What day of the week is it to-day ?	今天禮拜幾	Cheent'e-enn lee-pi chee?
To-day is Saturday	今兒禮拜六	Cheer lee-pi layo.
I want a button put on here	這兒要釘一個鈕子	Cher yow ting yeeka new-o-dza.
What's the time now ?	現在幾點鐘	Shendzi chee te-enn-choong ?
He (or it) is in the verandah	在廊子底下	Dzi lahngdza teeseeah.
Open the drawer	把抽屜拉開	Pah ch'o-t'ee lah-k'i.
The butter is all melted	黃油都化咯	Hwong-yo to hwahla.
Bring a small stool	擎一個小橙子	Nah yeeka sheeow tung-dza.
Take a feather brush and dust	擎担子担一担	Nah tahndza tahn-e-tahn.
Bring me a duster	擎一塊綻布來	Nah yeek'wi chahnpoo li
There's no lamp-oil	沒有燈油	Mayo tung yo.
Light a candle	點一枝臘燭	Te-enn yee chirp lah cho.
This table-cloth must be washed	這個台布要洗一洗	Chayka t'i-poo yow shee-e-shee.
Are there any matches ?	有取燈兒沒有	Yo ch'ü-tunger mayo?
This napkin must be changed for a clean one	這個手巾要換新的	Chayka sho-cheen yow hwahn sheenty.

THE SPORTSMAN.

Where's my gun?	我的鎗在那兒	*Woaty ch'eeang dzi nar?*
Is it loaded?	裝了藥沒有	*Chwongla yow mayo?*
Are there any snipe here?	這個地方有水鴜沒有	*Chayka tee-fahng yo shooey-jah mayo?*
Are there any pheasants?	有野雞沒有	*Yo yaychee mayo?*
This is a muzzle-loader	這個是前門的	*Chayka shirt ch'e-enn-munty.*
Breech-loaders are more convenient than muzzle-loaders	後門比前門好	*Ho-mun pee ch'e-enn-mun how.*
How much is this worth?	這個賣多少錢	*Chayka mi toa show ch'e-enn?*
I don't want to sell it	我不賣	*Woa poo mi.*
How d'ye do? (Lit., Have you had rice?)	吃了飯沒有	*Ch'irp lo fahn mayo?*
Can you let me sleep here?	我在這兒睡覺好不好	*Woa dzi cher shooey-cheeow, how poo how?*
I can't find my boat	我的船我找不着	*Woaty ch'wahn, woa chow-poo-chow.*
To-morrow I'll give you five taels	我明天給你五兩銀子	*Woa mingt'e-enn kay nee woo layang yeendza.*
I didn't hit that bird	那個鳥我沒打着咯	*Nahka neeow, woa may tah-chowla.*
Lend me a skin coat	你借我一個皮袄	*Nee cheeay woa yeeka p'ee-ow.*
Don't be afraid!	別怕	*Peeay p'ah!*
It's snowing outside	外頭下霜	*Wi-t'o seeah-seeay.*

It's fearfully cold	冷的利害	*Lungta-lehi.*
I can't sleep outside	我不能在外頭睡	*Woa poo nung dzi wi-t'o shooey.*
Send a man to find my boat	打發一個人找我的船	*Tahfah yecka ren chow woaty ch'wahn.*
I'll wait here	我在這兒等着	*Woa dzi cher tungja.*
When will you come back?	你多咯回來	*Nee toa-dzahn hooeyli?*
Have you a pipe?	你有烟袋沒有	*Nee yo yen-ti mayo?*
I want to smoke	我要吃煙	*Woa yow ch'irp yen.*
Bring the powder and shot	拏鎗藥來	*Nah ch'eeang-yow li.*
Is there an inn about here?	這個地方有客店沒有	*Chayka tee-fahng yo k'aw-te-enn mayo?*
Call the landlord	叫掌櫃的來	*Cheeow chahng-kwayty li.*
Are you the landlord?	你是掌櫃的麼	*Nee shirt chahng-kwaytyma?*
I want to take off my clothes	我要脫衣裳	*Woa yow t'oa ceshahng.*
Are there any wild-boar about here?	這個地方有野猪沒有	*Chayka tee-fahng yo yaychwo mayo?*
I am going into Mongolia (outside the great wall)	我要出口	*Woa yow ch'oo k'o.*
The hwong-yahng is found outside the Great Wall	口外有黃羊	*K'o-wi yo hwong-yahng.*
The road is very bad	道兒不好走	*Tower poo how dzo.*

GENERAL.

What is your honourable name?	貴姓	*Kway shing?*
Have you a wife?	你有夫人沒有	*Nee yo foo-ren mayo?*
What is your age?	貴庚 你多大歲數兒	*Kway kung; (to an inferior) Nee toa tah sooey-shoor?*
My humble name is Moo	我敝姓穆	*Woa pee shing Moo.*
I am 45 this year	我今年四十五	*Woa chin-ne-enn sir-shirt-woo.*
My wife is dead	我的婦人死咯	*Woaty foo-ren sirla.*
I have 4 sons	我有四個兒子	*Woa yo sirka urdza.*
I have no daughters	我沒有女孩兒	*Woa mayo nü-har.*
This is my son	這個是我的兒子	*Chayka shirt woaty urdza.*
How long have you been in China?	你在中國幾年	*Nee dzi Choongkwo chee ne-enn?*
What is your honourable nation?	貴國是那一國	*Kway-kwo shirt nah-yee kwo?*
Lend me five dollars	你借我五塊洋錢	*Nee cheeay woa woo k'wi ch'e-enn.*
I have no money	我沒錢	*Woa may ch'e-enn.*
I'll pay you to-morrow	我明天還你	*Woa mingt'e-enn hwahn nee.*
Give him six taels	給他六兩銀子	*Kay t'ah layo layang yeendza.*
One tael, five mace, three candareens	一兩五錢三分	*Yee-layang, woo ch'e-enn, sahn fun.*
Seven candareens are not enough	七分不殼	*Ch'ee fun poo ko.*
I have been 10 years in China	我在中國十年	*Woa dzi Choongkwo shirt ne-enn.*

Who came just now?	剛纔有甚麼人來	Kahng-ts'i yo shummo ren li?
Good-bye, good-bye	請請	Ch'ing, ch'ing.
I'll see you again to-morrow	明天再見	Mingt'e-enn dzi che-enn.
I want to buy some curios	我要買古董兒	Woa yow mi koo-toonger.
What do you want to buy?	你要買甚麼	Nee yow mi shummo?
I want to buy some enamel	我要買潑藍	Woa yow mi fah-lahn.
Enamel is very dear	潑藍狠貴	Fah-lahn hun kwey.
How much?	多少錢	Toa show ch'e-enn?
This isn't mine	這個不是我的	Chayka pooshirt woaty.
What nonsense!	甚麼話	Shummo hwah!
You're a fool	你是一個糊塗人	Nee shirt yeeka hoot'oo ren.
Don't you be cursing people	你別罵人	Nee peeay mah ren.
I must give you a thrashing	我要打你	Woa yow tah nee.
You are a bad man	你不是好人	Nee pooshirt how ren.

GRAMMAR.

SUBSTANTIVES AND ADJECTIVES

Are not declined: the same word expresses both the
singular and plural.

PRONOUNS.

I, me	我	*Woa.*
My, mine	我的	*Woaty.*
We, us	我們	*Woamun.*
Our, ours	我們的	*Woamunty.*
Thou, thee *and* you	你	*Nee.*
Thy, thine, your, yours	你的	*Neety.*
You (plural)	你們	*Neemun.*
Your, yours	你們的	*Neemunty.*
He, she, it, him, her	他	*T'ah.*
His, her, hers, its	他的	*T'ahty.*
They, them	他們	*T'ahmun.*
Their, theirs	他們的	*T'ahmunty.*

VERBS

remain the same in all moods, tenses, numbers and persons, with the exception of the past tense, which is formed by adding *la, layow* or *kwo* to the original word.

To come	來	*Li.*
I have come	我來咯	*Woa li-la.*
Has he come?	他來了沒有	*T'ah li-la mayo?*
He will not come	他不來	*T'ah poo li.*
Will he come?	他來不來	*T'ah li poo li*
They cannot come	他們不能來	*T'ahmun poo nung li.*
You (plural) needn't come	你們不用來	*Neemun poo yoong li.*
Don't you come!	你別來	*Nee peeay li!*

VOCABULARY.

A.

Accounts, to do	算賬	*Swahn jahng.*
Again	再	*Dzi.*
Ague, to have	發瘧子	*Fah yowdza.*
All	都	*To.*
Almonds	杏仁	*Shing-ren.*
Also	還要	*Hi yow.*
Alum	白礬	*Pi-fahn.*
Amah	老媽兒	*Lonmar.*
Anchor	錨	*Mow.*
Answer	回信	*Hwey sheen.*
Animal	牲口	*Shungk'ow.*
Anything	甚麼	*Shummo.*
Apple	檳菓	*P'ingkwo.*
Apricot	杏兒	*Shinger.*
Apron	圍裙	*Way-ch'ün.*
Arrowroot	藕粉	*O-fun.*
Ask, to	問	*Wun.*
Ask leave of absence, to	告假	*Kow cheeah.*
Asparagus	龍鬚菜	*Loong-shü-ts'i.*
Astracan	黑子羔	*Haydza-kow.*

B.

Bad	不好	Poo how.
Bag	口袋	K'ow ti.
Baggage	行李	Shinglee.
Bake	烤	K'ow.
Bale (of goods)	疋	P'ee.
Ball	球	Ch'ew.
Bar (of a river)	欄江沙	Lahn-chceang-shah.
Basket	筐子	K'wongdza.
Bath	澡盆	Dzow p'un.
Bathe	洗澡	Sheedzow.
Be, to	在，是	Dzi; shirt.
Because	因爲	Yeenway.
Bed	床	Ch'wong.
Bedclothes	被窩	Paywoa.
Bedroom	睡覺的屋子	Shooeycheeowty woodza.
Beef	牛肉	New-ro.
Beef-fat	牛油	New-yo.
Beef-steak	牛肉脾	Newro-p'i.
Behind	後頭	Ho-t'o.
Bend (of a river)	河灣	Haw-wahn.
Besides	另外	Ling wi.
Betel-nut	檳榔	Ping-lahng.

B—continued.

Bill	賬目	Jahng-moo.
Bird	鳥	Necow.
Bite, to (as a dog)	咬	Yow.
Black	黑	Hay.
Blacking	黑水	Hay shooey.
Black-lead	黑麪	Hay me-enn.
Blanket	毡子	Chahndza.
Blow, to (as wind)	颳	Kwah.
Blow out, to (as a lamp)	吹	Ch'ooey.
Blue	藍	Lahn.
Board	板子	Pahndza.
Boat	船	Ch'wahn.
Boatman	船戶	Ch'wahnhoo.
Boiling	開	K'i.
Book	書	Shoo.
Book-case	書架子	Shoo-cheeahdza.
Boots	靴子	Shüaydza.
Borrow, to	借	Cheeay.
Bottle	瓶子	P'ingdza.
Box	箱子	Sheeangdza.
Boy	跟班的	Kunpahnty.
Bread	麪包	Me-enpow.

B—*continued.*

Breakfast	早飯	*Dzow fahn.*
Brick	磚	*Chooahn.*
Bricklayer	瓦匠	*Wah-cheeang.*
Bridle	嚼子	*Cheeowdza.*
Bring	拏來	*Nah li.*
Broad	寬	*K'wahn.*
Broad bean	散荳	*Sahn-to.*
Bucket	水筲, 水桶	*Shooey - show ; shooey-t'oong.*
Bundle	包服	*Powfoo.*
Burn, to	燒	*Show.*
Butter	黃油	*Hwong-yo.*
Buttons	釦子	*New-o-dza.*
Buy, to	買	*Mi.*

C.

Cabbage	白菜	*Pi-ts'i.*
Cabin	客艙	*K'aw ts'ahng.*
Cake	餑餑	*Baw-baw.*
Calico	洋布	*Yahng-poo.*
Call, to	叫	*Cheeow.*
Camphor	樟腦	*Ch'ownow.*

C—*continued.*

Can do	可以	K'awyee.
Can, a	壼	Hoo.
Candareen	分	Fun.
Candle	臘	Lah.
Cap	帽子	Mowdza.
Captain	船主	Ch'wahn-choo.
Care, to take	小心、留心	Sheeow sheen; layo sheen
Cargo	貨物	Hwaw woo.
Cargo-boat	駁船	Paw ch'wahn.
Carpenter	木匠	Moo-cheeang.
Carpet	毯子	T'ahndza.
Carrot	紅羅蔔	Hoo lawbaw or hoong lawbaw.
Cart	車	Ch'aw.
Cash	錢	Ch'e-enn.
Cat	猫	Mow.
Catty	斤	Cheen.
Celery	青菜	Ch'ing-ts'i.
Certain	一定	Yee ting.
Chair	椅子	Yeedza.
Chair, sedan	轎子	Cheeowdza.
Charcoal	炭	T'ahn.
Chestnut	栗子	Leedza.

C—*continued.*

Chicken	小雞子	*Sheeow cheedza.*
Child	小孩子	*Sheeow hi-dza.*
Chimney	烟筒	*Yen-t'oong.*
Chinese	中國	*Choongkwo.*
Chop, to	劇開	*Toa k'i.*
Chow-chow, to have	吃飯	*Ch'irp fahn.*
Cigar	烟捲兒	*Yen-chüar.*
Clean	乾淨	*Kahnching.*
Clever	明白	*Ming-pi.*
Clothes	衣裳	*Eeshahng.*
Clove	丁香	*Ting-sheeang.*
Club, the	打球房子	*Tah-ch'ew-fahngdza.*
Clumsy	笨	*Pun.*
Coal	煤	*May.*
Cobweb	塲灰，蜘蛛網	*T'ah - hwey; chirpchoo-wang.*
Cold	冷	*Lung.*
Collar	禰子	*Lingdza.*
Comb, a	梳子	*Shoodza.*
Comb, to	梳	*Shoo.*
Come, to	來	*Li.*
Commissioner of Customs.	稅務司	*Shooey-woo-sir.*

C—*continued.*

Compass, a	定南針	*Ting-nahn-chun.*
Compradore	買辦	*Mi-pahn.*
Consulate	領事官衙門	*Ling-shirt-kwahn yah-mun.*
Cook, a	廚子	*Ch'oodza.*
Cook-house	廚房子	*Ch'oo-fahngdza.*
Copper	銅	*T'oong.*
Corkscrew	螺絲	*Lawsaw.*
Cotton (on reel)	線	*Se-enn.*
Cotton-wool	棉花	*Me-enn hwah.*
Cover, a	蓋兒	*Kar.*
Cover, to	街上	*Ki-shahng.*
Crack, to	裂	*Leeay.*
Crack, a	璺	*Wun.*
Crab	螃蟹	*P'ahng-seeay.*
Crease	摺兒	*Chawr.*
Crisp	脆	*Ts'ooey.*
Cucumber	黃瓜	*Hwong-kwah.*
Cupboard	櫃子	*Kweydza.*
Curtain	帳子	*Chahngdza.*
Cushion	椅墊子	*E te-endza.*
Customs	海關	*Hi-kwahn.*
Cut, to	刺	*Lah.*

D.

Darn, to	縫	Fung.
Day	天	T'e-enn.
Dead	死咯	Sirla.
Dear	貴	Kooey.
Devil	鬼子	Kweydza.
Dirty	膮臡	Ah-dzah or ahng-dzahng
Do, to	做	Dzoa.
Doctor	大夫, 醫生	Ti-foo or eeshung.
Dog	狗	Ko.
Dollar, one	一塊洋錢	Yee k'wi ch'e-enn.
Donkey	騾	Lü.
Door	門	Mun.
Double up, to	疊起來	Teeay-ch'ee-li.
Down	下	Seeah.
Draughty	透風	T'o fung.
Drawer	抽屜	Ch'o-t'ee.
Drink, to	喝	Haw.
Duck	鴨子	Yahdza.
Duck, wild	野鴨子	Yay yahdza.
Dust, to	擔一擔	Tahn-e-tahn.
Duster	毡布	Chahn-poo.
Dye, to	染	Rahn.

E.

Ear	耳朶	Urta.
Earrings	鉗子	Ch'e-endza.
East	東	Toong.
Eat, to	吃	Ch'irp.
Ebb-tide	落潮	Low-ch'ow.
Egg	鷄子兒	Cheedzer.
Employ	用	Yoong.
Ended	完咯	Wahnla.
English	英國	Yingkwo.
Enough	彀	Ko.
Ermine	銀鼠	Yeen-shoo.
Evening	晚上	Wahnshahng.
Every	每	May.
Eyes	眼睛	Yenjing.

F.

Face	臉	Layenn.
Fair (of wind)	順	Shoon.
Fall, to (of things)	掉下	Teeow-seeah.
Far	遠	Yüahn.
Fast	快	K'wi.

F—*continued.*

Fat (1) of people; (2) of meat	胖, 油	(1) *P'ahng;* (2) *yo.*
Father	父親	*Foock'in.*
Fear, to	怕	*P'ah.*
Feather-brush	担子	*Tahndza.*
Feed, to	餵	*Way.*
Fetch, to	拏來	*Nah li.*
Fever and Ague, to have	發瘧子	*Fah yowdza.*
Few	少	*Show.*
Fight, to	打架	*Tah cheeah.*
Filter, to	過淋	*Kwo leen*
Fine, to	跑, 罰, 扣	*P'ow; fah; k'o.*
Finger-bowl	玻璃碗	*Pawly-wahn.*
Finished	完咯	*Wahnla.*
Fire	火	*Hwaw.*
Fire-wood	劈柴	*P'ee-ch'i.*
First, the	頭一個	*T'o-yeeka.*
Fish	魚	*Yü*
Flea	蛇蚤	*Kawdza.*
Flood-tide	漲潮	*Chahng ch'ow.*
Floor	地板	*Tee-pahn.*
Flour	麪, 白麪	*Me-enn; pi me-enn.*
Flower	花兒	*Hwar.*

F—*continued.*

Flower-pot	花盆	*Hwah-p'un.*
Fly, a	蒼蠅	*Ts'ahng-ying.*
Foot, a	脚	*Cheeow.*
Foot, a (in measure)	尺	*Ch'irp.*
Fork	錘子	*Ch'ahdza.*
Foreign	外國	*Wi-kwo.*
Fox	狐狸	*Hoolse.*
French beans	扁荳	*Pe-en-to* or try *pe-ennto.*
Fresh	鮮	*Se-enn.*
Freeze, to	凍	*Tvong.*
Fry, to	扎	*Jah.*
Fruit	菓子	*Kwo-dza.*
Full	滿	*Mahn.*
Fur	皮, 皮子	*P'ee* or *p'eedza.*

G.

Gauze-window	紗壁子	*Shah-peedza.*
Get up, to	起來	*Ch'ce-li.*
Ginger	薑	*Cheeang.*
Girth	肚帶	*Too-ti.*
Give, to	給	*Kay.*

G—continued.

Gloves	手套	Sho-t'owr.
Go, to	走	Dzo.
Go round, to	轉	Chooahn.
Go out, to	出門	Ch'oo mun.
Goat	山羊	Shahn-yahng.
Godown	棧房	Jahn-fahng.
Gold	金, 金子	Cheen or cheendza.
Good	好	How.
Goose	鵝, 鴈	Aw; (wild) yen.
Glass, a	玻璃	Pawly.
Grapes	葡萄	P'oot'o.
Grate, to	砸碎	Dzah sooey.
Green	綠	Lil.
Grey shirtings	洋布	Yahng-poo.
Guest	客	K'aw.
Gun	鎗	Ch'ceang.
Gunboat	兵船	Ping-ch'wahn.

H.

Hair	頭髮	T'o-fah.
Hair (of fur)	毛	Mow.
Hair-brush	刷子	Shwahdza.

H—*continued.*

Half	一半	Yee pahn or yee par.
Halter	籠頭	Loongt'o.
Ham	火腿	Hwoa-t'ooey.
Hammer	銀頭. 錘子	Lahngt'o; ch'ooydza.
Hand	手	Sho.
Handkerchief	絹子. 手巾	Chüandza; sho-cheen.
Hang up, to	掛起來	Kwah-ch'ee-li.
Hard	硬	Ying.
Hare	野猫	Yaymow.
Hat	帽子	Mowdza.
Have, to	有	Yo.
He	他	T'ah.
Head	腦袋	Now-ti.
Hear	聽	T'ing.
Hem, to	蹺	Ch'eeow.
Here	這兒	Cher.
Hire, to	僱	Koo.
Hold, the	艙	Ts'ahng.
Home, at	在家. 家裡	Dzi cheeah; cheeahlee.
Honey	蜂蜜	Fungmee.
Hong	行	Hahng.
Horse	馬	Mah.

H—*continued.*

Horse-radish	辣根	*Lah-kun.*
Hot	熱	*Raw.*
House	房子	*Fahngdza.*
How?	怎麼	*Dzummo?*
How much? how many?	多少. 幾個	*Toa show? checka?*
Hungry	餓	*Aw.*

I.

I	我	*Woa.*
Ice	氷	*Ping.*
Ice-box	氷箱子	*Ping-sheeangdza.*
Ice, to	振着 振着	*Chunja chunja.*
Ill, to be	有病. 不舒服	*Yo ping; poo shoo-foo.*
In there, etc.	那裡. 那裡頭	*Nah-lee or nah-leet'o.*
Inch	寸	*Ts'oon.*
Indian-corn	棒子	*Pahngdza.*
Ink	墨	*Maw.*
Inside	裡頭	*Leet'o.*
Inside out	裡兒朝外. 面兒朝裏	*Leer ch'ow wi; me-er ch'ow lee.*
Instance, for	比方	*Pee-fahng.*
Invite, to	請	*Ch'ing.*

I—*continued.*

Iron	鐵	*T'eeay.*
Iron, an	烙鐵	*Lowt'ee.*
Iron, to	熨開	*Yün-k'i.*

J.

Jacket	小褂子, 馬褂	*Sheeow kwahdza; mah-kwah.*
Jade	玉	*Yü.*
Jetty	馬頭	*Maht'o.*
Jug	壺	*Hoo.*

K.

Keep, to	留下	*Layo-seeah.*
Kettle	水壺	*Shooey-hoo.*
Key	鑰匙	*Yowsh.*
Kidney	腰只	*Yowdza.*
Kill, to (chickens, etc.)	宰	*Dzi.*
Kind (sort)	樣子	*Yahngdza.*
Knife	刀子	*Towdza.*
Knot (to tie)	擊個扣兒	*Cheeka-k'or.*
Know, to	曉得, 知道	*Sheeowta; chirp-tow.*

L.

Lamp	燈	*Tung.*
Lantern	燈籠	*Tung-loong.*
Large	大	*Tah.*
Late	晚	*Wahn.*
Lazy	懶惰	*Lahntaw.*
Leaf of a tree	樹葉子	*Shoo yaydza.*
Leak, to	漏	*Lo.*
Leather	皮, 皮子	*P'ee* or *p'eedza.*
Left hand	左手	*Dzoa sho.*
Lemon	香櫞	*Sheeang-yüan.*
Lend, to	借	*Cheeay.*
Less	少	*Show.*
Let go, to	鬆, 鬆手	*Soong; soong sho.*
Letter	信	*Sheen.*
Lid, a	蓋兒	*Kar.*
Lie, to	撒謊	*Sah-hwong.*
Lie down, to	躺下	*T'ahng-seeah.*
Light (not heavy)	輕	*Ch'ing.*
Light, to	點	*Te-enn.*
Lightning, thunder and	雷閃	*Lay-shahn.*
Like	像	*Sheeang.*
Like, to	喜歡, 愛	*Shee-hwahn; i.*

L—*continued.*

Lime	灰、白灰	*Hwey; pi hwey.*
Little, a	少	*Show.*
Little (not big)	小	*Sheeow.*
Liver	肝兒	*Kar.*
Lock, to	鎖	*Saw.*
Long	長	*Ch'ahng.*
Look, to	看、瞧	*K'ahn; ch'eeow.*
Looking-glass	鏡子	*Chingdza.*
Lucky	有造化	*Yo dzow-hwah.*

M.

Mace	錢	*Ch'e-enn.*
Make, to	做	*Dzoa.*
Make haste !	快快	*K'wi k'wi!*
Man	人	*Ren.*
Many	多、好些個	*Toa; how sceayka.*
Maskee	不要緊	*Poo yow cheen.*
Mast	桅杆	*Way-kahn.*
Master	東家	*Toong-cheeah.*
Matches	取燈兒	*Ch'ü-tunger.*
Matting	蓆、篷子	*Shee; p'ungdza.*

M—*continued.*

Medicine	藥	*Yow.*
Melon	香瓜	*Sheeang-kwah.*
Melon, water	西瓜	*Shee-kwah.*
Mend, to	收拾	*Sho-shirt.*
Middle	中間兒	*Choong-che-er.*
Milk (cow's)	牛奶	*New ni.*
Mince, to	切碎	*Ch'eeay sooey.*
Mint	百合	*Pawhaw.*
Monday	禮拜一	*Lee-pi yee.*
Month	月	*Yüay.*
Money	錢	*Ch'e-enn.*
Moon	月	*Yüay.*
Mop	敦布	*Toon-poo.*
Morning	早起	*Dzow-ch'ee.*
Mosquito	蚊子	*Wundza.*
Mosquito-curtains	蚊帳	*Wunjahng.*
Mother	母親	*Mooch'in.*
Mouse	耗子	*Howdza.*
Mouth	口、嘴	*K'o, or tsooey.*
Much	多	*Toa.*
Mushroom	蔴菰	*Mawkoo.*
Must	得	*Tay.*

M—continued.

Mustard	芥末	*Cheeayman.*
Mutton	羊肉	*Yahng-ro.*
Mutton-chop	羊牌骨	*Yang p'i-koo.*
My	我的	*Woaty.*

N.

Nail, a	釘子	*Tingdza.*
Nail, to	釘上、釘釘	*Ting-shahng; Ting ting.*
Name	姓、名字	*Shing; mingdza.*
Narrow	窄	*Chi.*
Needle	針	*Chun.*
New	新	*Sheen.*
Night	夜、黑下	*Yay; hay-secah.*
North	北	*Pay.*
Nose	鼻子	*Pecdza.*
Notes (of money)	票子	*P'ecowdza.*
Now	現在	*Shendzi.*
Nutmeg	荳蔲	*To k'o.*
Nutmeg-grater	硒椿	*Dzah-chwong.*

O.

Office	寫字房	*Seeaydzafahng.*
Oil	油	*Yo.*
Old (clothes)	舊	*Chew.*
Old (applied to people)	老	*Low.*
Old (stale)	陳	*Ch'un.*
On the bed	床上	*Ch'wong-shahng.*
Onion	葱	*Ts'oong.*
Open, to (a door)	開	*K'i.*
Open, to (a box)	打開，撬開	*Tah-k'i; (if nailed down) ch'ecow-k'i.*
Opium	洋藥	*Yahng-yow.*
Orange	橘子，橙子	*Chüdza; ch'undza.*
Ounce	兩	*Layang.*
Outside	外頭	*Wi-t'o.*

P.

Pane of glass, a	一塊玻璃	*Yee k'wi pawly.*
Paper	紙	*Jilt, or jump.*
Partridge	沙鷄	*Shah chee.*
Paste	漿子	*Cheeangdza.*
Paste, to	糊	*Hoo.*
Pattern	樣子	*Yahngdza.*

P—*continued.*

Pay, to	給錢, 還錢	*Kay ch'e-enn; hwahn.*
Peach	桃	*T'ow.*
Pear	梨	*Lee.*
Peas	灣荳	*Wahn-to.*
Pecul, a	一担	*Yee tahn.*
Peking	北京	*Pay-ching.*
Pen	筆	*Pee.*
Pencil (lead)	鉛筆	*Ch'e-enn pee.*
Pepper	胡椒麪兒	*Hoo-checow-me-er.*
Persimmon	柿子	*Shirtdza.*
Pheasant	野雞	*Yay-chee.*
Pick up, to	揀起來	*Che-enn-ch'ee-li.*
Piece	塊	*K'wi.*
Piecee	個	*Ka* or *kaw.*
Pigeon	鴿子	*Kawdza.*
Pillow	枕頭	*Chunt'o.*
Pilot	引水的	*Yeen-shooeyty.*
Pin	浲瘩針	*Kawter-chun.*
Pincushion	針毡兒	*Chun-cher.*
Place	地方	*Tee-fahng.*
Plate	盤子	*P'ahndza.*
Play, to (as children)	玩兒	*Wahr.*

P—*continued.*

Plum	李子	*Leedza.*
Poach, to (eggs)	窩	*Woa.*
Pocket	口袋	*K'ow-ti.*
Pony	馬	*Mah.*
Pork	猪肉	*Choo-ro.*
Port, a	海口	*Hi-k'ow.*
Potato	山藥荳兒	*Shahn-yow-tor.*
Pound	斤	*Cheen.*
Pour, to	倒	*Tow.*
Pudding	點心	*Te-ensheen.*
Pull out, to (a drawer)	拉開	*Lah k'i.*
Pull, to	拉	*Lah.*
Push, to	推	*T'ooey.*
Put, to	擱在	*Kawdzi.*

Q.

Quality	成色	*Ch'ungsaw.*
Quick	快	*K'wi.*
Quince	木瓜	*Mookwah.*

R.

Rabbit	兔子	T'oodza.
Races	跑馬	P'ow mah.
Race-course	跑馬廠	P'ow-mah ch'ahng.
Rain; (2) it rains	雨、下雨	Yü; (2) Seeah yü.
Raisins	葡萄乾兒	P'oot'o kar.
Ready, it is	得咯、預備好	Tawla; yüpay howla.
Ready made	現成兒的	Shen-ch'ung-er-ty.
Red	紅	Hoong.
Relation	親戚	Ch'een-ch'ee.
Rice (cooked)	飯、白米飯	Fahn or pi-mee fahn.
Rice (uncooked)	白米	Pi mee.
Ride, to	騎	Ch'ee.
Right (to be)	有理	Yo lee.
Right (hand)	右手	Yo sho.
Ripe	熟	Sho.
River	河	Haw.
Road	道兒、道路	Tower; tow-loo.
Roast, to	烤	K'ow.
Robe	外套兒	Wi-t'ower.
Room, a	屋子	Woodza.
Rope	繩子	Shungdza.

R—continued.

Round	圓	Yüan.
Rub, to (in cleaning)	擦	Ts'ah.
Run, to	跑	P'on.
Run, to (in needle-work)	執針兒工	Chirp-cher-koong.

S.

Sable	貂鼠	Teeowshoo.
Saddle, a	鞍子	Ahndza.
Salt	白鹽	Pi yen
Salt-beef	鹹牛肉	Se-enn newro.
Saturday	禮拜六	Lee-pi layo.
Saucepan	鍋	Kwo.
Say, to	說	Shoo-o.
Scorpion	蝎子	Seeaydza.
Scissors	剪子	Che-endza.
Screw	螺絲	Lawsaw.
Sea-otter	海虎	Hi-foong.
Sea-sick, to be	暈船	Yün ch'wahn.
See, to	看，看一看	K'ahn; k'ahn-e-k'ahn.
Seek, to	找	Chow.
Sell, to	賣	Mi.

S—continued.

Send, to (a man)	打發、送	*Tahfah;* (a thing) *soong*
Separate	單	*Tahn.*
Servant	跟班的	*Kunpahnty.*
Several	幾個	*Cheeka.*
Sewing-silk	絮線	*Shü se-enn.*
Shake, to (clothes)	抖擻	*Tolo.*
Sheet	被單	*Pay-tahn.*
Shoe	鞋	*Seeay.*
Shoe, to (a horse)	釘掌	*Ting jahng.*
Shop	舖子	*P'oodza.*
Short	短	*Tvoahn.*
Shrimp	蝦米	*Seeahmee.*
Shut, to	關、關上	*Kwahn; kwahn-shahng.*
Sick (ill)	不舒服	*Poo shoo-foo.*
Silk	綢子	*Ch'owdza.*
Silver	銀子	*Yeendza.*
Sing	唱曲	*Ch'ahng.*
Sit, to	坐	*Dzoa.*
Skin	皮子	*P'ee* or *p'eedza.*
Slow	漫	*Mahn.*
Slowly	漫漫的	*Mahn-mahnty.*
Smoke	烟	*Yen.*

S—*continued.*

Smoke, to (of a chimney)	冒烟	*Mow yen.*
Sneeze, to	打嚏噴	*Tah t'ee-fun.*
Snipe	水鴷	*Shooey-jah.*
Soap	胰子	*Yeedza.*
Soak, to (1) in hot water, (2) in cold	發開，泡開	(1) *Fah-k'i;* (2) *p'ow-k'i*
Sock	襪子	*Wahdza.*
Soda	鹼	*Che-enn.*
Soft	軟	*Rooahn.*
Solder, to	釬上	*Hahn-shahng.*
Sole (fish)	鰨默魚	*T'ahma yü.*
Son	兒子	*Urdza.*
Soot	烟煤子	*Yen-maydza.*
Sort	樣子	*Yahngdza.*
Soup	湯	*T'ahng.*
South	南	*Nahn.*
Spade	鐵鍫	*T'ee-ay ch'eeow.*
Spider	蜘蛛	*Chirp-choo.*
Spinach	菠菜	*Paw-ts'i.*
Spectacles	眼鏡兒	*Yen-jinger.*
Sponge	海磨	*Hi-maw.*
Sponge-cake	蛋糕	*Tahn-kow.*

S—*continued.*

Spoon	勺子、匙子	*Showdza; ch'irpdza.*
Spread, to	舖	*P'oo.*
Square	四方的	*Sir fahngty.*
Squirrel	灰鼠	*Hwey-shoo.*
Stable	馬號、馬棚	*Mah-how; mah-p'ung.*
Stale	陳	*Ch'un.*
Starch	漿子	*Cheeangdza.*
Start, to	起身	*Ch'ee shun.*
Steamer	火輪船	*Hwaw-loon ch'wahn.*
Steersman	舵工	*Toa-koong.*
Stew	膾	*Hwey.*
Stick, a	棍子	*Koondza.*
Stirrup	馬鐙	*Mah-tung.*
Stool	櫈子	*Tungdza.*
Stop up, to	杜住	*Too-choo.*
Stove	爐子	*Loodza.*
Stow away, to	貯穩	*Chwong.*
Strainer	罩籬	*Chowlee.*
Straw	草	*Ts'ow.*
String	繩子	*Shungdza.*
Sugar	白糖	*Pi t'ahng.*
Sun	太陽	*T'i-yahng.*

S—continued.

Sun-stroke, to have	晒咯	Shi-la.
Sunday	禮拜	Lee-pi.
Sweet (to smell)	香	Sheeang.
Sweet (to taste)	甜	T'e-enn.

T.

Table	棹子	Chawdza.
Table-cloth	台布	T'i-poo.
Tael	兩銀子	Layang yeendza.
Tail (of a Chinaman)	辮子	Pe-endza.
Tail (of an animal)	尾巴	Ee-pah.
Tailor	裁縫	Ts'i-fung.
Take, to	拏	Nah.
Take away, to	撤去	Ch'aw-chü.
Take down, to (pictures, etc.)	摘下來	Chi-seeah-li.
Tape	帶子	Ti-dza.
Tea	茶, 茶葉	Ch'ah; (in the leaf) ch'ah-yay.
Tea-cup	茶碗	Ch'ah-wahn.
Tea-pot	茶壺	Ch'ah-hoo.
Telescope	千里眼	Ch'e-enlee-yen.

T—*continued.*

Tell, to	告訴	*Kursoo.*
Tender (meat)	嫩	*Nun.*
That	那個	*Nahka.*
Then	那個時候	*Nahka shirt-hor.*
There	那邊 那兒	*Nahpe-enn; nar.*
Thermometer	寒暑錶	*Hahn-shoo peeow.*
They	他們	*T'ahmun.*
Thick (of liquids)	稠	*Ch'o.*
Thick (of substances)	厚	*Ho.*
Thimble	頂針兒 頂針的	*Tingcher; ting-chunty.*
Thin (not fat)	瘦	*Sho.*
Thin (not thick, of liquids)	稀	*Shee.*
Thin (of substances)	薄	*Pow.*
Thing	東西	*Toongshee.*
Think, to	想	*Sheeang.*
Thirsty	渴	*K'aw.*
This	這個	*Chayka.*
Thunder	雷	*Lay.*
Thursday	禮拜四	*Lee-pi sir.*
Tiger	老虎	*Lowhoo.*
Time	時候	*Shirt-hor.*

T—*continued.*

Tin	馬口鐵	*Mahk'a t'eeay.*
Tinker	鑛碗的	*Chü-wahnty.*
Toast	烤麪包	*K'ow me-enpow.*
To-day	今兒, 今天	*Cheer; chint'e-enn.*
Together	一塊兒	*E-k'war.*
Tomato	火柿子	*Hwaw-shirtdza.*
To-morrow	明兒, 明天	*Meer; mingt'e-enn.*
Tongue	舌頭	*Shawt'o.*
Too much *or* to many	太	*T'i.*
Towel	手巾	*Sho-cheen.*
Towel-horse	手巾架子	*Sho-cheen cheeahdza.*
Tray	盤子	*P'ahndza.*
Treacle	糖水	*T'ahng-shwoey.*
Tree	樹, 樹木	*Shoo; shoo-moo.*
Truth	寳話	*Shirt-hwah.*
Tub	篓, 澡盆	*Lo; (bath) dzow-p'un.*
Tuck in, to	壓底下	*Yah tee-seeah.*
Tumbler	玻璃砵	*Pawly-pay.*

U.

Umbrella	雨傘	*Yü-sahn.*
Under	底下	*Tee-seeah.*
Underdone	生不熟	*Shung; poo sho.*
Understand	懂得	*Toongta.*
Unpick, to	拆開	*Ch'i-k'i.*
Unripe	不熟	*Poo sho.*
Untie a knot, to	解開扣兒	*Cheeay-k'i k'or.*
Use, to	用	*Yoong.*
Useful	有用處	*Yo yoong-ch'oo.*

V.

Vegetable	素菜	*Soo-ts'i.*
Vegetable-marrow	菜瓜	*Ts'i-kwah.*
Very	狠	*Hun.*
Vinegar	醋	*Ts'oo.*

W.

Wages	工錢	*Koong ch'e-enn.*
Wait, to	等, 開飯	*Tung;* (at table) *k'ifahn*
Walk, to	走	*Dzo.*
Wall	墻	*Ch'eeang.*

W—continued.

Walnut	核桃	*Haw-t'ow.*
Want, to	要	*Yow.*
Warm	煖和、熅和	*Nooahnhaw;* (of water, etc.) *wunhaw.*
Wash, to	洗	*Shee.*
Washerman	洗衣裳的	*Shee eeshahngty.*
Watch, a	錶	*Peeow.*
Water	水	*Shooey.*
Wear, to	穿、戴	*Ch'wahn;* (of hats) *ti.*
We	我們	*Woamun.*
Week	禮拜	*Lee-pi.*
Weigh, to	約一約、稱一稱	*Yow-e-yow; ch'ung-e-ch'ung.*
Well, a	井	*Ching.*
Well (in health)	好	*How.*
West	西	*Shee.*
What?	甚麽	*Shummo?*
When?	多喒	*Toa-dzahn?*
Where?	那兒	*Nar?*
Whip, a	鞭子	*Pe-endza.*
White	白	*Pi.*
Who?	誰	*Shooey?*
Whole	整	*Chung.*
Why?	爲甚麽	*Way shummo?*

W—continued.

Wide	寬	K'wahn.
Wind	風	Fung.
Window	窻糊	Ch'wonghoo.
Wine	酒	Cheeoo.
Wine-glass	酒砳	Cheeoo-pay.
Winter	冬天	Toong t'e-enn.
Wolf	狼	Lahng.
Woman	女人	Nü-ren.
Wood	木頭	Moot'o
Work, to	作活	Dzoa hwaw.
Write, to	寫	Seeay.
Wrong, you are	你錯咯	Nee ts'oa-la.
Wrong (not the right one)	不對	Poo tooey.

Y.

Year	年	Ne-enn.
Yeast	肥、麪肥	Fay; me-enfay.
Yellow	黃	Hwong.
Yesterday	昨天	Dzoa t'e-enn.
You	你、你們	Nee; (plural) neemun.
Young man, a	年輕的	Ne-enn ch'ingty.
Your	你的、你們的	Neety; (plural) neemun-ty.

Second Edition, Revised and Greatly Enlarged.

3 Volumes, Royal 4to., **$15.00**

語言自邇集

TZŬ ÊRH CHI;

BY

Sir THOMAS FRANCIS WADE

AND

WALTER C. HILLIER.

A PROGRESSIVE COURSE

DESIGNED TO ASSIST THE STUDENT OF

COLLOQUIAL CHINESE

as spoken in the Capital and the Metropolitan Department.

VOL. I.

Prefaces.—Memorandum for the Guidance of the Student.—Pronunciation.—The Radicals.—Chinese Text of "The Forty Exercises," etc., "The Ten Dialogues," "The Hundred Lessons," "The Graduate's Wooing," "The Tone Exercises," and "The Parts of Speech." 379 pp.

VOL. II.

English Translations of "The Forty Exercises," etc., "The Ten Dialogues," "The Hundred Lessons," "The Graduate's Wooing," "The Tone Exercises," and "The Parts of Speech" (with copious Explanations and Notes). 530 pp.

VOL. III.

Glossary of Words and Phrases.—Index of Characters, arranged according to Radicals.—The Peking Syllabary.—Writing Exercises. 251 pp.

LEAVES FROM MY CHINESE SCRAP-BOOK.

BY

FREDERIC HENRY BALFOUR.

$3.00.

CONTENTS.

NEW I. M. CUSTOMS PUBLICATIONS.

General Tariff for the Trade of China. $0.50.

Returns of Trade at the Treaty Ports and Trade Reports for the year 1886.   Part I, $1.00; Part II, $5.00.

Returns of Trade for the Treaty Ports.
Separate returns for each port.   50 cents each.

Customs Gazette.
No. LXXIII, January–March 1887. $1.00.

List of Chinese Light-houses, Light-vessels, Buoys, and Beacons for 1887.   Fifteenth Issue. $1.50.

Medical Reports for the half year ending 31st March 1887.   33rd Issue. $1.00.

Royal 4to., *319 pp.*, **$6.00.**

COURS ÉCLECTIQUE
GRADUEL ET PRATIQUE
DE

LANGUE CHINOISE PARLÉE

PAR

C. IMBAULT-HUART.

TOME PREMIER,

COMPRENANT

I.—Une Introduction à l'Étude de la Langue Chinoise.
II.—Les Principes Généraux de la Langue Chinoise Parlée.
III.—Six Appendices se rapportant à ces Deux Parties de l'Ouvrage.

PAR LE MEME AUTEUR.

Recueil de documens sur l'Asie Centrale.
Traduits du Chinois. 8vo., avec cartes. $5.00.

Les Instructions Familières du Dr. Tchou Po-Lou.
Traite morale pratique publie avec deux traductions française, etc. 8vo. $2.00.

Anecdotes, Historiettes et Bons Mots en Chinois Parlé.
Publiés pour la première fois avec une Traduction Française et des notes.
12mo. $0.75.

La Legende du Premier Pape des Taoistes.
Et l'histoire de la famille pontificale des Tchang. 12mo. $2.00.

Manuel de la Langue Chinoise Parlée à l'usage des Français. 12mo.
                                                            $2.00.

La Poésie Chinoise du XIVᵉ au XIXᵉ Siècle.
Extraits de Poëtes Chinois. Traduits pour la première fois.   75 cts.

RECENT PUBLICATIONS RELATING TO

CHINA & THE FAR EAST.

Mayers' Chinese Government.
A MANUAL OF CHINESE TITLES, CATEGORICALLY ARRANGED AND EXPLAINED, WITH AN APPENDIX.
Second Edition, with Additions by G. M. H. PLAYFAIR. $3.00.

List of the Higher Metropolitan and Provincial Authorities of China.
Compiled by WALTER C. HILLIER.   Corrected to December 31st, 1886. $1.00.

Journal of the Peking Oriental Society.
Vol. I., No. 4.   50 cents.

The Middle Kingdom.
A SURVEY OF THE GEOGRAPHY, GOVERNMENT, LITERATURE, SOCIAL LIFE, ARTS, AND HISTORY OF THE CHINESE EMPIRE AND ITS INHABITANTS.
By S. WELLS WILLIAMS, LL.D. Revised Edition, with Illustrations and a New Map of the Empire.   2 vols. $10.50.

Leçons Progressives pour l'Etude du Chinois Parlé et Ecrit.   Par A. MOUILLESAUX DE BERNIÈRES. $3.00.

Deutsch–Chinesisches Conversationsbuch.
Nach JOSEPH EDKINS' PROGRESSIVE LESSONS IN THE CHINESE SPOKEN LANGUAGE.   Von JOSEPH HAAS. $3.50.

Text-Book of Documentary Chinese.
With a Vocabulary.   Edited by F. HIRTH, PH.D.   Vol. 1.   Demy 4to., 280 pp.
$2.00.

China and the Roman Orient.
RESEARCHES INTO THEIR ANCIENT AND MEDIÆVAL RELATIONS AS REPRE-SENTED IN OLD CHINESE RECORDS.   By F. HIRTH, PH.D. $3.00.

John Chinaman's Bamboo Tree.
Illustrated.   By Mrs. CLEMENT F. R. ALLEN. $1.00.

Some of the Analects of Confucius.
Illustrated by Mrs. CLEMENT F. R. ALLEN. $3.00.

Translation of the Peking Gazette for 1886. $2.00.

A General View of Chinese Civilization, and of the Relations of the West with China.

From the French of M. PIERRE LAFFITTE (Director of Positivism); translated by JOHN CAREY HALL, M.A. $1.00.

Mémoires concernant l'Histoire Naturelle de l'Empire Chinois.

Par DES PÈRES DE LA COMPAGNIE DE JÉSUS. Vol. II, Part. I. $2.00.

Fâ-Hien's Record of Buddhistic Kingdoms.

(A.D. 399-414). Translated and annotated with a Corean Recension of the Chinese Text, by JAMES LEGGE, M.A., LL.D. $4.00.

A Book on Chinese Games of Chance.

By NG KWAI-SHANG. $2.00.

Japanese Fairy Tales Told in English.

By B. H. CHAMBERLAIN. 14 Books already issued ; 20 cts. each or 6 for $1.00. Edition on Crépe paper, 25 cts. each or 5 for $1.00.

Die Einnahmequellen und der Credit Chinas.

Nebft Uphorismen über die Deutsch-ostasiatischen Handelsbeziehungen von U. H. EXNER. $1.00.

A Muramasa Blade.

A Story of Feudalism in Old Japan. By LOUIS WERTHEIMBER.
In Padded Silk Cover. $6.50.

Some Chinese Ghosts.

By LAGCADIO HEARN. With Appendix, Notes, and Glossary. $1.25.

The Land Question.

With Lessons to be drawn from Peasant Proprietorship in China. By JOHN DUDGEON, M.D., C.M., Peking.   50 cents.

Pirie's Original Conversations in English and Japanese.

Part I.   50 cents.

Keeling's Guide to Japan.

Together with Useful Hints, History, Customs, Festivals, Roads, &c., &c. *Third Edition*, with maps. $2.00.

PUBLICATIONS

OF THE

CATHOLIC MISSION AT ZI-KA-WEI.

---◆---

METEOROLOGICAL WORKS BY PÈRE DECHEVRENS.

Le Typhon du 31 Juillet 1879.
In 4°, pages 55, plates 8. $3.00.

The Typhoon of July 1879.
In 4°, pages 23, plates 4. $2.00.

On the Storms of the Chinese Seas and on the Storm of the 19th March 1880.
In 4°, pages 16, plates 3. $1.00.

The Typhoons of the Chinese Seas in the year 1880.
In 4°, pages 34, plates 2. $1.00.

The Typhoons of the Chinese Seas in the year 1881.
In 4°, pages 176, plates 5. $3.00.

Les Typhoons de 1882.
1ère Partie—Juillet et Août. In 4°, pages 53, plates 7. $2.00.

The Typhoons of the year 1882.
2nd Part—September-November. In 4°, pages 32, plates 2. $1.00.

The Typhoons of the Chinese Seas in the year 1885.
With an Essay on the Atmospheric Variations during January 1885.
In 4°, pages 42, plates 18. $3.00.

Récherches sur les Variations régulières des Vent à Zi-ka-wei, 1877.
In 4°, pages 25, plates 8. $1.00.

La Lumière Zodiacale étudiée d'après les observations faites de 1875 à 1879 à Zi-ka-wei.
In 4°, pages 38, plates 2. $1.00.

Sur l'inclinaison des Vents; nouvelle girouette pour observer cette inclinaison, etc.
Première note. In 4°, pages 31, plates 9. $1.00.

Le magnétisme terrestre à Zi-ka-wei, Chine.
In 4°, pages 53, plates 13. $2.00.

Instructions in the Use of Meteorological Instruments.
In 12°, pages 67, plates 8. $1.00.

Instructions for Keeping the Meteorological Log.
In 4°. $1.00.

The Meteorological Elements of the Climate of Shanghai.
Twelve years of observations made at Zi-ka-wei. In 8°, pages 37. $0.50.

Memoires concernant l'Histoire Naturelle de l'Empire Chinois.
Vol. I., Parts 1, 2 & 3. Each $5.00.
Vol. II., Part 1. $2.00.

COUVREUR (L. P. S.)—*Dictionnaire Français-Chinois.*
Contenant les expressions les plus usitées de la Langue Mandarine.
1,034 pp., Demy 8vo. $7.00.

Guide de la Conversation Français-Anglais-Chinois. $2.50.

HEUDE (R. P.)—*Conchyliologie Fluviatile de la Province de Nanking et de la Chine Centrale.*
Numerous Plates. Royal 4to. Parts 1 to 8. Each $3.00.
Part 10. $5.00.

Method for Learning to Read, Write and Speak English.
For the Use of Chinese Pupils. Three Parts. $5.00.

HOANG (PETER.)—*A Notice of the Chinese Calendar, from 1624 to 2020. And a Concordance with the European Calendar.* $2.50.

De Calendario Sinico et Europæo, 1624–2020.
De Calendario Sinico Variæ Notiones. Calendario Sinici et Europæi Concordantia. De Calendario Ecclesiastica. $3.00.

Meteorological Register for use on the Coast of China. $1.00.

ZOTTOLI (P. A.)—*Emmanuelsis Alvarez Institutio Grammatica ad Sinensis Alumnos Accomodata.* $3.00.

Bulletin Mensuel de l'Observatoire Magnétique et Météorologique de Zi-ka-wei. Published annually. Each $3.00.

REDUCED IN PRICE.

ZOTTOLI (P. A.)—*Cursus Literaturæ Sinicæ.*

Vol. 1.—Pro Infima Classe Lingua Familiaris.
2.—Pro Inferiore Classe Studium Classicorum.
3.—Studium Canonicorum.
4.—Pro Suprema Classe Stylus Rhetoricus.
5.—Pars Oratoria et Poetica.

Single Volumes, $7.00 each. The Set of 5 Vols., $25.00.